Fog Lane

Fog Lane

by Neil Campbell

Chapeltown Books

British Library Cataloguing in Publication Data

A Record of this Publication is available from the British Library

ISBN 978-1-910542-08-8

This edition published 2017 by Chapeltown Books
Manchester, England

Some of these stories first appeared (in slightly different form) in *The Best of CaféLit 5*, *Flash Frontier*, *Funny in Five Hundred*, *Ink, Sweat and Tears*, *Orbis*, *Poetic Diversity*, *Spelk*, *The Shelagh Delaney Collection* and *Welsh Arts Review*. Thanks to the editors.

DEDICATION

For Nom

Thanks to David Gaffney for the inspiration, to Danny Moran for his feedback on earlier drafts of the stories, and to Simon Buckley for the wonderful cover photo. Finally, thanks to Gill James for helping this book see the light of day.

Not what happens there but the there itself.

Karl Ove Knausgaard

CONTENTS

INTRODUCTION

Fog Lane is a collection of stories about memory. Many of the stories have been published online and in magazines. They were written over a long period of time. The oldest, *The Rose Garden* was first written in about 2007 and published in *Orbis*. The last one in the book, *Here Comes the Sun* was completed just recently. I think of them as short shorts. I dislike the term flash but you can also call them that. What I love about the story form is that you can write in a great variety of styles and from many different points of view. The stories in this book vary from the humorous to the sad to the macabre. I have always preferred stories where the meaning is inferred through symbolism and metaphor. Plot is secondary for me. I find plot boring even if I sometimes use it. These are the best short stories of under a thousand words I've written in the last ten years.

Neil Campbell
January 2017

THE SUN IN SEPTEMBER

Corned Beef went to his local in Burnage to ease himself out of the day with pints of bitter. For years, he did this until at one stage he began to see scratches on his face in the bathroom mirror in the morning. Usually they were on his forehead but sometimes on his cheeks. He washed away the thin lines of dried blood and then got on the 197 to work as usual.

The scratches began to develop into cuts and one morning he woke to see blood across the pillow. He felt for his forehead and his forefinger squished into a gash. He went to the bathroom mirror and took a plaster from the cabinet, placing it across his forehead. In work that day, below a staircase in a dark chamber within the neo-gothic splendour of Manchester Town Hall, he sat with the other porters at break time drinking coffee from his flask.

'Hey, Corned Beef,' said Bungalow, 'what's with the fucking plaster?'

'Cut me head.'

'How did you manage that?'

'Don't know.'

Sometimes Corned Beef went into work with so many plasters on his face that he looked like he'd been involved in an explosion. The people in shiny shoes who clattered up and down the town hall stairs avoided eye contact. When he stood outside in the shadow of the great clock tower smoking his Park Drive, he looked across the rain dampened concrete of Albert Square towards the memorial that was covered in pigeon shit.

The man with his face covered in plasters was a familiar sight for the regulars of The Sun in September, and if anyone came into the pub and asked about it they were told, oh, that's just Corned Beef, as though that answered the question.

Eventually Corned Beef woke with blood seeping from his eyes. He tilted his head back and walked to the bathroom and felt around in the cabinet for two more plasters. Squinting into the bathroom mirror, eyes dripping, he wiped one eye and then the other, before walking the familiar route to Burnage Lane.

GHOST CLASS

It was a bit of a hike to get there: two trains and a bus. So, I set off in the dark. When the inter-site bus stopped near the campus I was the only one to get off. In bed the night before I had had envisioned Oxford Road in Manchester, where thousands of students crowd the scene. I walked down the street that led to the campus, past the playing fields where the netting in the football goals waved in the wind. I walked through the car park, the only sound the brushing of brittle leaves across tarmac.

I navigated the maze of corridors and went into the associate lecturers' office. There were three unattended computers. There was a note on one of the desks with my name on it. Underneath that was a list of names. I made myself some coffee and then looked at my lesson plan. I had read the primary text the previous afternoon and felt confident of answering questions on it.

At two minutes to ten I left the office. I locked it behind me with the key I'd been given and walked upstairs to the classroom. On the stairs, I looked out of the window at the netting in the football goals waving in the wind. There was nobody going up or down the stairs. And there was nobody in the corridor or waiting outside any of the rooms. I walked to the end of the corridor and saw the door of the classroom. It was next to the fire escape. I felt the bunch of nerves in my stomach that suggested I would be on my game. I waited a split second and then pushed open the door. The tables and chairs were arranged in a semi-circle. But there was nobody sat at the tables.

A massive sense of anti-climax flooded through me as I looked down at my lesson plan. I flicked through the primary text in another futile gesture. I looked up at the clock on the wall at the far end of the room. Maybe they were all still on their way.

After half an hour, I picked up my stuff and wandered over to the administration block. I had been told that Mary Macintosh was the woman to ask if I was ever stuck with anything. I went into her office. There was a bell on the desk and I rang it. There was movement behind frosted glass and Mary appeared. She asked if she could help me. I said yes, I was supposed to be teaching 10-12 in A57. She asked me my name and the subject I was teaching. Then she went to her computer and looked at the screen for a few minutes. She said there were no seminars timetabled in A57 that morning. She asked me what subject I was teaching. And then she asked me my name again.

HOUSE AT DUSK

I've been writing this book. I was determined to avoid anything autobiographical, and have done, until now. I'm house-sitting for a friend of mine. What Rick didn't realize is that I tried to give up drinking. With a warm heart, he left a cold fridge stocked copiously with bottles of Chimay, a strong and lovely beer brewed by Trappist monks.

I haven't stopped drinking since I came here. I found more cases of Chimay in various parts of the house, then a box of Cobra beer, and then I started on the wine. There were six boxes of Sauvignon Blanc, with six bottles in each. I've had the bottle of malt whisky, three bottles of Shiraz and a bottle of Absolut vodka.

I don't have any money and the booze is running out so I've started selling things. First thing to go was the big TV. I went into the Fletcher Moss and sold it within fifteen minutes. I had a pint in there, and then went to the off licence for a box of Tiger. Most of the rest of the house is filled with books and CDs and you don't really get much for them. I tried to sell the mannequins but nobody was interested. Then I realized the cat was some kind of pedigree and found someone on the internet to buy it.

Rick and family are still in New York, where he's teaching. I have a month left. I was sure one of the neighbours would contact him. I sold lampshades, bathroom fittings, the kids' toys, wardrobes, chests of drawers, the bed in the main bedroom, coffee tables, couches, the fridge freezer, the washing machine, bookcases, binoculars, clothes (his and hers), the satellite dish, old issues of literary magazines. I've been chopping up the decking for the wood fire. When that went, I started throwing the books on. I'm drinking Cobra, just Cobra now, nothing else. India's finest.

All that's left in the house besides a single bed and this

laptop are the mannequins. Two in the front window, a man and a woman, hand in hand, naked. Upstairs two children, side by side, naked. In the guest room where I sleep, a woman with no hands, naked. The plastic torso and head of a pretty woman looks down on me as I write this. She is naked too, but for the makeup. Looking in the windows and seeing the silhouettes, you might be forgiven for thinking they were real.

THE FORD

There was a moment of driving rain that forced him into a grouse butt for some semblance of shelter, and he huddled there, his woolly hat on under the hood of his waterproof jacket and his gloved hands tucked deep into coat pockets. As the rain battered down he kicked at a few spent cartridges.

There was an old cart track that ran in loops down the hillside and passed between two twinned lakes. A gaggle of Greylag geese began an infernal honking as he passed. Soon he could see down to the A road and the handful of houses huddled around the church that constituted the village. The clouds shifted and bathed the valley in golden sunlight, and as he came down off the higher ground, Blaine felt himself warming up, and soon he dropped his hood and took off his hat and unzipped his coat to his chest. At the farm gate, he saw the golden crescent of the river sweeping past the old hall. It was only when the water levels were high that you could see the river from the farm gate.

He knew he shouldn't bother but the shortcut across the ford cut off a good two miles. Otherwise he had to walk all the way down to the footbridge and then come back again through the village. As Blaine approached the water he scrutinized the crossing point. He walked up and down the embankment and though he could see through the water to where the farmer had piled the bricks and stones it was too deep. On the opposite bank, he could see the scars of the tractor tracks going up the bank, but they were old tracks, deep-grooved from years of use. There was a sign on the fence: 'Private Fishing Only'.

'Too deep!' shouted a voice. 'Go away! Too deep!'

Blaine looked around and saw a man that he had previously imagined to be his father. He stood in wader's waist deep in the water with a golden line dipping from a rod into the river. He then started waving his hand in a motion that suggested Blaine move back.

'I'll fucking decide if it's deep enough,' Blaine muttered under his breath. He couldn't be arsed shouting above the noise of the fast-flowing water. Nobody owns the fucking river, thought Blaine, and he stood there staring at the man. Then he leaned against the fence post where it said 'Private Fishing Only' and took out his map to look at the point on it where the ford was marked. Hopefully that would shut him up.

There were always fisherman driving their 4x4's behind the house to go night fishing. Even when it was totally freezing outside. This seemed like madness to Blaine, who had never been taught to fish.

Blaine had been on the booze and his whole face felt red from both that and sitting in the garden all afternoon. The old house was good for keeping cool in summer but it had been so hot for the last couple of weeks that he needed to go outside again. There was enough of a breeze to keep the midges off and he sat in the lawn chair drinking in the glow of the outside light. When he finished his bottle of Wainwright ale he stood up to go for another and then an idea took hold of him.

He made his way down the old road that went down to the railway track and followed the path under it into the field where all his neighbours walked their dogs. He made his way down to where the tractor tracks scarred the embankment. He could hear oystercatchers and curlews in the darkness. The coldness of the river water was blissful as it filled his shoes. The moonlit sweep of the river rippled and sighed. He made his way across and sat on the bank until a light breeze licked his wet pants and made him feel cold. He looked upriver and there was a blackened figure in the water, standing below the hills in the moonlight.

DICTIONARY JESUS

Along the top floor corridor lads queued outside the classrooms smashing each other over the head with bags or getting each other into headlocks or banging each other's heads on the walls. Latecomers ascended the 'Up' stairs. A lad called Bobby Hankinson vomited spray cream in the playground and the evidence was covered by sawdust.

Because of the vomiting Bobby got to his classroom late. The queue had filtered into the room and all the lads sat in their chairs looking up at Mr Bullows. When Bobby came in he tried to just go to his seat but Bullows called him up to the front. Bullows took an empty chair from the front row and turned it around so that it faced the class. He told Bobby to stand on the chair. Bobby stood on the chair. He told Bobby to hold his arms out wide. Bobby held his arms out wide.

Bobby had seen it happen before but hadn't always laughed as loudly as the others. And he bitterly regretted that third cream cake. This wouldn't be the last time that his sweet tooth got him into trouble.

Bullows went to the bookshelf for the dictionaries. He carried a big pile of them and put them on to his own desk. Then he put one dictionary onto each of Bobby's upturned hands. Immediately Bobby's arms began to sag with the weight and he grimaced towards the ceiling. The laughter was already uproarious as Bullows put another dictionary onto each of Bobby's hands. With this weight Bobby's arms fell and the books collapsed onto the floor.

SPADEWORK

Kevin Bell was known as Bell-End. It seemed the most appropriate use of his surname. When we got changed for rugby practice it was noisy with the sounds of studs on the tiled floor. We ran out following Mr Ward onto the soaking wet fields in the rain. As a way to warm up, the lads got together in pairs. I stood completely still as Paul McCormack ran up and tackled me. When it was my turn I ran at him full tilt in revenge and took off, tackling him somewhere around the chest. There was a nice soft landing in the mud. Five minutes of this and we were all warmed up for the game.

We lined up along the touchline. We all wore red rugby shirts. Half of us took them off and turned them inside out so they were blue. The wind was swaying the uprights. Brett Swainbank was on the blues side and we therefore won by fourteen tries to nil, Brett scoring all fourteen tries. We just gave him the ball and then stood around in the rain watching him hurtle towards the distant try line. Sometimes he'd just put the ball down with one hand. Other times he'd dive full length to slide pointlessly and joyously across the rain-slicked grass.

In the dressing room after the game Bell-End started throwing the bits of grass and mud from the underside of his boots. Then everyone else started doing it. Then Bell-End caught one in the eye from Brett Swainbank. Swainbank was just one of those kids who were good at everything. There were great roars of ribald laughter as Bell-End clutched at his muddied eye. Bell-End threw his boots at Swainbank in revenge. But his timing was bad. Mr Ward had just come in at that moment.

We all went silent. Bell-End was told by Mr Ward to bend over. He did. And Mr Ward whacked him on the arse with a spade. Everyone burst out laughing. But Bell-End didn't get up from the floor. I think someone later said that the spade had hit his cock, which confused me at the time.

VIEWINGS AVAILABLE

We had been looking at properties in the High Peak for as long as I could remember. We had been gazumped more than once. This particular Saturday afternoon, we went to a property in Furness Vale.

First impressions were good: nice little front garden, solid looking front door complete with stained glass window. A morose looking man with greasy grey hair answered the door and let us in. Inside it felt like stepping off a plane in Spain. A coal fire blazed in the inglenook and a fan on top of the fire circulated the heat throughout the house.

'Nice and warm in here,' said my wife.

'Can be,' said the man, 'bloody draughty though.'

He led us into the kitchen. There were lovely fitted units, and plenty of room for the large dining table. 'Gets bloody cold in here,' he said.

'Can we have a look upstairs?' said my wife.

'Aye. Murder these stairs. But come on.'

'Is it just you here then?' I said, on the way up.

'Yeah, just me. The wife's under the patio.'

'Two bedrooms or three?' said my wife.

'I'm showing you now. You can count them for yourself if you like.'

'Three,' I said.

'Well, no actually. You're wrong there,' he said, with something approaching glee. 'It's two and a half. You can't get a bed in that one.'

'Right.'

We wandered in to the front bedroom. There was a splendid view of the Peak District countryside, with horses on the hillside and jackdaws flying.

'Nice view,' I said.

'It is today. But how many days do we get like this?' he said, running fingers through his greasy grey hair.

As I tried to ignore the sight of clothes on the bedroom floor there was a shocked expletive from my wife. 'Don't go in there,' she said, pointing to the bathroom. '*Do not* go in there.'

'There's a nice shower,' I said, looking for positives.

'It really doesn't matter. We have seen more than enough.'

We hastened down the stairs. When the man opened the front door he gave me a greasy handshake.

Passing the FOR SALE sign in the front garden we got in the car. Traffic went by on Buxton Road and the red 199 pulled up outside The Soldier Dick.

'What kind of person would do that?' said my wife, starting the engine.

ROOMS FOR TOURISTS

The rookery overlooked the rooms. A naturalist had once counted over five hundred nests. The rooks went *kah kah kah* every day. The few people who stayed in the rooms usually didn't come back, I guess because of the noise. But some people liked it and one man in particular returned every autumn, said he loved watching the flight of the birds in the sky. In the vale, there were not only rooks, but other species of Corvus: jackdaws, carrion crows, one or two pairs of ravens. It had taken me a while to work out the differences.

At breakfast, he would eat everything we put before him, and after spreading marmalade on his toast and drinking his tea he would start to flick through the RSPB handbook. He had the binoculars on the table next to the tea pot. He would rarely speak but always smiled and we were always glad to see him. On days of especially bad weather he liked a bath when he returned and I was always happy to run it.

When I was making the beds, I'd look out through the bedroom windows and watch him as he made his way across the hillside to a vantage point. He always sat for at least a couple of hours as the day moved through pastel colours to dusk. He knew when they would fly by in their swirling congregations, and sometimes I'd watch it too, through the windows. And I'd look at him sitting there in all weathers, the binoculars pressed to his eyes, tracing the birds across the sky.

I watched from the window as the man came back year after year; saw each year in the morning light at the breakfast table how he'd aged. I wondered why he'd never been married.

One day when I ran his bath I took my clothes off and stood before him. I was shy about my falling figure but I had to do it. I washed him in the bath, soaped him gently and he sat there in a rapture of pleasure as though my breasts were the birds and the sky.

Even before my mother died we began to run the rooms for tourists together. He was a good cook and happy to make the breakfast every morning, and in the autumn of every year we went out onto the moors and hillsides together at dusk to watch the black flight of rooks, jackdaws, carrion crows and ravens. In the white sheets of our bed we'd press our warm bodies together and listen to the *kah kah kah* of rooks in the rookery, all five hundred nests filling the silences of the country air, giving definition to the landscape, calling forth the old poetries of the land. And as the numbers of rooks seemed to increase and estimations of the nests reached towards the thousand mark, the number of tourists increased, and birdwatchers filled our rooms for most of the year.

Then in some semblance of a nightmare, some intimation of their departure, I heard one almighty *kah kah kah* in the night, as though they were all calling together. We went out to look for them, but the skies were silent and the trees had all been cut down. It was though you could hear the grass growing, or flickering in the wind at least, but the landscape seemed like a field of corn after a tornado. I once read how a man in a tropical clime ventured out after a hurricane and a hundred hummingbirds landed on his hat.

My daughter is old enough now so we run the rooms together, though few people ever come, just one man who never speaks but who we think is working for the government. Every day after breakfast he goes out alone and I watch from the bedroom windows as he walks across the green fields and looks up at the empty skies and the saplings.

MY OLD MAN

In winter his hands curled into clenches. He'd sit in his chair by the living room window looking across the Blackbrook Valley. I preferred the view from the kitchen. We were at the foot of Chinley Churn, so close that you'd think if a stone fell from the summit it could land on our slate roof. There was a path that came down off the top and I could see people walking down it on a Sunday. There were jackdaws and crows in the air above them; sometimes, on clear sunny days, buzzards in the blue sky. I always heard the buzzards before I saw them; it was their pained whistles that led me to look up. It was the same with ravens; their deep croak in contrast to the more common calls of crows or the sociable chirruping of jackdaws. Dad liked the dippers in the river.

Once the next-door neighbour was having some work done on his house and had the skip dropped right in front of ours. This meant we had to park further down Stubbins Lane.

'He could have asked us first,' said Dad.

'Maybe they just dropped it there.'

'Funny how he left room for his car.'

'Well it won't be there long, will it?'

'That's not the point, all he had to do was come and knock on the door. Is it not bad enough that he wakes us up every morning?'

'The man is obviously not well.'

'I'm going to stick his head down that toilet one day.'

'Dad, I doubt he'll be around much longer.'

'He'll be coughing away for years. Quicker to do myself in. Why don't you just tip me in that skip and have done with it?'

'Come on, Dad, don't be daft.'

Sometimes Dad asked me to take him down Charley Lane to look at the mill where he'd worked for so many years.

'Ironic, isn't it,' he said, the last time. 'Most of the people I worked with came out of there stone deaf. I wish I was stone deaf then I might get some kip.'

We were standing on the bridge by the Black Brook that ran past the walls of the mill. The mill had been converted into flats and some were some still available. There were midges around the river and I thought that if I lived there I would never open a window. But the light on the ripples of the river had something nice about it, and there was a dipper down there.

THE ANGEL OF THE BRIDGE

There's a curve of the river down near the golf course where, on a warm summer evening, all the trivialities of the suburbs disappear beneath the surface of sunlight sparkling on water.

One such summer night, I took Barney around the curve of the river and there were dippers dipping from stones. Dozens of geese lined the grassy banks. Magpies and crows flitted in the trees of the golf course, and there were more crows by the riverside. The green iron footbridge that led across from the allotments and the parking area to the golf course was backlit by the descending sun. That sunlight sprinkled the flight of midges, and the wings of swallows that spiralled across the surface of the water to catch them.

He was standing there, also backlit by the sun, the man I should have married, flicking out his hair so that it seemed suffused with flame. The shy eyes that could make me cry were glistening at the sight of the swallows. Barney always barked at him and he always just smiled in return. We walked side by side around the curve of the river, our feet leaving footprints in sand. We followed the path off the river and through the park. We didn't talk because we didn't have to. Sitting on a memorial bench together he told me once again the names of the surrounding flowers and trees. As the dusk came down we sat closer, and when it got colder we stood up and walked past the fading lines on the tennis court. The calls of birdsong were lost to the traffic as we went our separate ways.

THE FACE

With one hand holding on for balance as the bus shunted and swayed down Oxford Road, she used the other to scrunch her bus ticket. Just before she got off, I could see that she had fashioned a swan.

A few months later I was at a friend's. His house was halfway up a hill and there was a great view across the valley towards the train station and the hillsides above it. We sat on the balcony drinking beer. When he went to the toilet I watched the flight of swallows across the sky. There was a golden light across the hills. When Robert came back out he showed me a book he was working on. It was a series of photographs and he had been asked to write accompanying haiku. They were of the same woman in various poses, and when I'd flicked through to the end I was convinced it was the woman I had seen on the bus.

Robert put me in touch with her via Facebook, and we arranged to meet for a drink. I waited and waited for her but she didn't turn up. I called a friend I hadn't seen for ages and he came out and carried on drinking with me. We crossed the road and went in The Metropolitan. The ale was good and I don't remember getting home.

It was mid-morning by the time I got up. Even the magpie calls hurt my head. A crow called too, from a treetop opposite, rocking back and forth as it did so, and finally another crow came and joined it. After Football Focus I managed to get down some noodles on toast and by mid-afternoon I was coming around. It wasn't until then that I thought of the woman who hadn't turned up. I looked on Facebook and couldn't find her anywhere. I lay on the couch thinking about her.

It was a year or more later that I opened a package and saw that Robert had sent me a copy of the book. A beautiful coffee table sized tome, it was filled with the same pictures I'd seen before, plus Robert's haiku. In one picture her face was whitened. This image returned to me in dreams.

I found her on Twitter. I was sure it was her face. She had reversed the letters of her surname. I followed her on Twitter and almost immediately she blocked me. Just like her Facebook page, her Twitter page was filled with images of her own face.

I think that moment on the bus was the only time I ever actually saw her. In our brief exchange on Facebook she never corroborated the origami thing. She never denied it either. But if it weren't for the haiku book I might doubt that she'd ever existed at all.

KIPPAX STREET

The 111 from Southern Cemetery took me down Burton
Road and then Yew Tree Road. I passed the training ground
at Platt Lane and got off the bus on Claremont Road where
I went into the chippy for a chip muffin. Beside me was a
portly old comedian with curly hair. While waiting for his
fish he did an impression of Popeye.

On Kippax Street, I knocked on the door of Tommy
Caton's place but he wasn't in, and I thought of his promise
and how he'd died so young. Big Joe Corrigan passed me on
the other side of the road, waving his gloved hands.

In the house next to Caton's, there was a woman
polishing the doorstep. She had long blonde hair and rang a
bell. Her name was Helen. I looked in her window and there
was a man with long grey hair who looked like the ghost of
John Gidman. There was an inflatable Fyffe's banana
floating in the sky over Maine Road. A man and his boy got
out of their car and gave 50p to a young lad to look after it.
The man took a bag of aniseed balls from his Parka pocket
and passed them to his son before lighting a Silk Cut.

I wondered how long it would be before Imre Varadi
turned up. Thinking of that I saw Alex Williams washing his
car and then stopping to stretch his back. I saw Ian
Brightwell on several occasions as he ran laps of the estate.
In the time I was on the street, Paul Moulden scored seven
goals in his back yard. Mark Lillis was celebrating in a silly
way and Gordon Davies gave him a sly look.

In the house next to Helen's, Jimmy Frizzell played
chess with Billy McNeill as Mel Machin and Brian Horton
knocked on the door. There was the smoke of John Bond's
cigar. They could hear disco music coming from Niall
Quinn's.

Ian Bishop passed elegantly. David White sped to the

scrapyard. Andy Hinchcliffe crossed over. Paul Stewart muscled his way past a loitering Imre Varadi. Then I saw two men pushing a broken-down Rolls Royce that had Trevor Francis behind the wheel. The two men were Steve Redmond and Neil McNab.

An ice cream van turned up. Eric Nixon did the driving and Perry Suckling passed the cornets. I asked for a 99 and Suckling dropped it. Andy Dibble was there too, and he got an ice cream but someone sneaked up behind him and stole it out of his hands. I think it was John Burridge, or it might have been the guy who played mainly for Ipswich and saved a lot of penalties, Paul Cooper.

I asked about Francis Lee but someone said he'd moved out and that they were praying he wouldn't come back. Georgi Kinkladze was there though, dribbling, and Tony Morley, brushing his grey moustache. Ricky Holden made his way slowly down the street as George Weah made a brief visit. Joe Royle was on his way back to Oldham. Howard Kendall and Peter Reid were going back to Everton. Reidy's hair was dyed black.

When Lakey answered the door, I told him how much I'd loved his book. I told him that he was the greatest player I'd ever seen and that he would have been the England captain. He slammed the door in my face. I would have liked to have told him how good he was, but instead I just thought of the times I'd seen him play, in those years after the youth team cup triumph over United, when he would waltz past several players with that upright running style of his. And his prowess in the air, his tackling, distribution, engine. What a player he was. And I wanted to say to him, well, Lakey at least you had your moments, those moments you were watched from the Kippax by so many thousands of men who would have given anything to play just a few minutes on that same pitch as you. To see that old stand with its corrugated roof from the pitch instead of from underneath, where we craned our necks around the stanchions. The stand where men thronged among the smoke of cigarettes, escaped their own minds for ninety minutes to shout and swear and scream and dream for the boys in blue like you. Lakey, you were one of them for a few years and they'll never take that away, and I'm sorry mate if your knee still hurts you as you twitch in the night for more comebacks.

Next door to Lakey there were several men comparing their grey moustaches: Jim Tolmie was there, and super Kenny Clements, and the mercurial Gerry Gow. Tommy Hutchinson was there too, having decided not to put a wall up in the yard. Mick McCarthy was shouting in his broad Barnsley accent. When they seemed to agree among themselves that Paul Power's tash was by far the best, Tony Grealish started kicking them. Neil McNab was here, there, and every fucking where. Then Tony Coton turned up and that put the cat amongst the pigeons, until, because of his subsequent role on the coaching staff at Old Trafford, he was disqualified. When Billy Meredith descended from the heavens, Power shook him by the hand and that was that.

YOUR SUPERMARKET

Every week Sarah drove down the hill to the supermarket in her 4x4. She browsed the shelves at leisure, her head filled with the soothing tones of the old Scouse poet on the advert. She filled her trolley to the brim with produce, half of which she would throw away at the end of the week.

One week the supermarket had to temporarily close. The automatic doors were opening and shutting of their own accord and a stray basket was being battered in the gap. Half-filled trolleys littered the darkening aisles as produce toppled onto the floors. Doris on the checkout felt lost in the moment and scanned her own hands in the fading light.

At home, our lady of the afternoons wept into scatter cushions. There was a knock on the door and the old Scouse poet came in and consoled Sarah with lines of rhyming verse, spontaneously composed at the sight of her brimming cupboards.

The next morning Sarah climbed trembling into her 4x4. She was tentative by the sliding doors. But when she went in they were playing Christmas songs: John Lennon, Slade, and Wham.

Doris was on the checkout, all smiling and jovial, no longer scanning her own hands. She felt filled with energy just a few days away from the moment when, weighed down with as many bottles of Rioja as she could afford with the staff discount, she would pass exultantly beyond the trolley boundaries on the outer edges of the car park.

FOR YOU

Coming up for you today we have interviews with some of the finest footballers of a generation. They will answer questions that we will put to them for you. The programme will be simultaneously broadcast on TV and radio and online and projected on the walls of the nearest castle just for you. We'll recap on the programme five minutes in for you, just in case you forget anything, and we'll show it again for you in one hour and then next week on a different channel. Adverts geared to you will tempt you with tempting offers just for you, the voiceovers and music adjusted to a higher volume for your listening pleasure.

After I've shared the programme with you, filled with self-serving quips of which I've become a master, and pointless forays across the iPad through which I'll share the inanities of the viewing public, I'll take my glazed eyes home and while watching myself on screen I'll blow my own fucking head off.

At breakfast time the follow morning, the news will be read from an autocue and the presenters will indicate their feelings on the topic through a wide range of sublimely irritating facial expressions.

ANOTHER GOOD COUNTRY

From our tent behind the Kingshouse we could see across the A82 and the pools of Glen Etive to the granite bulk of Buachalle Etive Mor. The loss of many years before returned more urgently to us as we climbed to the summit of the mountain once again. We fed bread to ravens before walking back down the mountain the way we came. Looking back, we saw the mountain rescue bothy standing alone on the valley floor. We stayed another night behind the Kingshouse and the next morning made our way through the mists along the A82 and into the broadening valley of Glencoe.

In Glencoe, we stayed at a place called the Red Squirrel campsite and in the evening went for a meal at the Clachaig Inn, perched snug in the valley below the bulk of the Aonach Eagach ridge. The climbers rattled their karabiners and sloshed down beer and got more boring by the minute.

The following morning, we drove further north, past the Kyle of Lochalsh and the Skye Bridge, with the jagged ridges of the Cuillin covered in mist above the Sound of Sleat. Further on we went, pushing memories back behind the accumulating slides of scenery. The first moment the Sat Nav said Assynt, our minds were filled with all our favourite MacCaig poems, and we drove onwards towards the north, where we planned to stay at Glencanisp Lodge and then take in the summits of Suilven, Canisp and Stac Polly.

THE STREET WITH NO NAME

The trains rattled above Corned Beef as he lay against the brick wall. He rose and reached for his cup, walking the streets and warming up and soon having enough for a coffee in the cafe where the man smoked cigarettes at the counter.

The streets were loud with the sound of traffic crashing through puddles in the rain. His eyes blurred with the rain and the streetlights spread across his vision in orange clouds. The revellers came click-clacking across the pavements. Groups of lads, groups of girls all came near him to get money out from the cash point. He saw then gripping fistfuls of twenties and folding and sliding them into purses and wallets. Most people said they had no change when he mumbled up towards them but plenty did. Some people passed the coins while others tossed them in his general direction. Several men told him to 'stop fucking begging and get a job', and one man reached down and grabbed his coat, lifting him from the ground before dropping him down again to the laughter of his mates.

Corned Beef went into the Spar. He didn't bother with a carrier bag and instead secreted the bottle within the folds of his long coat, walking the familiar route back to the street with no name.

THE FLIGHT OF THE CONDOR

Daniel got off the bus at Monterey and bought himself a bottle of wine. He sat drinking it on a bench near the statue of Ed Ricketts. He walked down Cannery Row and saw where Ricketts had lived, the observatory where he analysed specimens collected from tide pools in the bay, the place where Steinbeck came to help him.

Daniel was drunk in California, looking down on Monterey Bay and hoping for the shadow of a whale. He stayed at a hostel and an older man offered to drive him along the Pacific Coast Highway. He took the chance to get closer to the home of Henry Miller but when the driver touched his leg Daniel got out.

He was left standing there on the Pacific Coast Highway and he didn't know which way to go. He walked over a barrier and stood on the edge of cliffs, watching the swells of the Pacific far below. A huge black bird passed over his head with an ugly pink face and a magnificent wing span. Daniel leaned back and watched it soaring.

An old lady crossed the highway. She'd been watching him from her chair on the porch.

'Do you like our birds?' she asked him.

'Yeah, what are they?'

'Condors. And they're in danger. That one up there, well she's almost sixty years old. But some of them fly into power lines and people still poison them and shoot them.'

The old lady welcomed him in for tea which she brought on a tray with cups and saucers. Her name was Alice. They sat at her table on the porch watching condors above the Pacific Ocean.

KOMAPSUMNIDA

Matthew had wanted to go to Japan but could only get an ESOL job in South Korea. He bought the Lonely Planet guide beforehand and looking at the map of the mountains close to Jinhae City kept all negative thoughts from his head.

His luggage was lost in transit. When he arrived at the airport in Busan he had to call the person who was supposed to be meeting him. When that person arrived, she drove him to an apartment block that was still being built. In his apartment, there was a lovely view of the mountains but no furniture. That night he was put in a hotel instead. There was a rack of pornographic films in the lobby and the hotel owner slept in his underpants on the floor behind the reception desk. All night there was the sound of high heels up and down the stone stairs, and a mosquito buzzing in his ear. He turned the light on and sat there naked and sweating, listening to the mosquito without being able to see it.

The next morning, he was shown around the school and the head teacher offered him rice cakes. They went to a restaurant that looked like a McDonald's but wasn't. The streets were unpaved. There were piles of rubble, broken tractors and low slung telephone wires.

When the teacher dropped him back off at the apartment block and left him there with a camp bed to sleep on, Matthew considered his options. He checked how much money he had and once his mind was made up that was it.

At home, he thought he had failed himself. What if he'd stayed the year? Maybe he could have adapted, maybe not. But that year in England he met the girl of his life, and when he took her to a Korean restaurant she was mightily impressed when he said thank you to the smiling waitress.

A WORN PATH

Twice a week Mary wheeled her trolley down the hill, over the railway crossing and along the canal to the big Tesco in Whaley Bridge. She said hello to the people she saw sitting on their narrow boats, and waved at the horses in the fields next to the sewage plant. She never liked the idea of living on a narrow boat, especially in winter, when the frozen water encased your home in ice. You could only ever go anywhere slowly and there would be all the locks to navigate. She continued along the towpath and under another footbridge giving access to Bridgemont and with a sign on it advertising a beer festival. At the canal junction near Whaley Basin she had to struggle across a little metal footbridge going over the water, and then down a small hill and through the car park.

Coming home was even more tiring because of the weight of the trolley and the walking already done. In all weathers of the High Peak she walked the towpath there and back to go shopping. She felt that it kept her strong. She could have got on the 199 with her bus pass, but that's how stubborn she was about getting her exercise. And the buses were full of old people and she hated talking to old people because all they ever talked about was being old.

The last time she went shopping the canal was frozen solid as she struggled along the towpath. The wheels of her trolley stuck time and again in the wind sculpted piles of snow. She struggled a final time at the trolley and fell face forward. At first she tried to get up but then she decided to stay there. After twenty-three years as a widow she could make that decision for herself.

The snow continued to fall and started coming down more heavily, so that by nightfall Mary and her trolley were fully covered over in thick snow. The temperature dropped sharply that night, encasing her in a frosted tomb. In the afternoon, a couple of teenagers who'd been cycling down the towpath starting jumping over the hump in the sunlight. Over and over they jumped, turning around, coming back and jumping again, until grey hair appeared through the melting snow.

MAQUIS

It was out of season at the tiny holiday resort but the following morning they made for the beach and sat there hypnotized by the crystal blue waters. They sat for three days, relaxing and running back to fat. On the third day, they looked along the beach and saw a channel cut through the sand with turds floating down to the sea. By the sand flecked road near the beach they could see their piles of pizza boxes and beer bottles.

In the blue sky, planes came in and out of the airport at Ajaccio. They remembered looking down at Corsica from the plane on their arrival and how they'd been shafted for taxi fare at the airport. Then they remembered the ten days in the mountains, walking with the subtle scent of maquis and standing above cloud inversions in a place that looked like heaven.

ENGLAND'S LAST WILDERNESS

It was on the high moorland between the North Pennines and Northumberland. On New Year's Eve, they walked around the village with their heads on fire and people came from miles around to see it. Becky and Rachel were just two of those that went to watch, jumping back from the head-tossed sparks of flame in the darkness and bitter cold.

At dusk the following day Becky and Rachel saw the vine covered dereliction of the old hotel and its faded sign. Skeletal trees reflected from the many windows. They were inquisitive and courageous women and so they wandered their way in through the darkness. In every room and on every bed, there were the perfectly preserved corpses of folk musicians, and on the ceilings of those rooms were their souls, as green and shifting as the northern lights.

It was an exhausting task, but Becky and Rachel stood on wobbling chairs with their long coats unbuttoned, reaching around the ceiling spaces to gather the souls of the folk musicians. With all the souls tight to their breasts they got in their little Citroen and drove the country roads home, keeping their long coats buttoned and the car windows closed.

THE CORPSE ROAD

He made chorizo in the red wine he'd carried from before Dufton and sat on rocks beside the tent in the dusk, watching the brightening headlights of cars on the B road between Ashgill and Alston. Finishing the wine, he returned to his tent, leaving the door unzipped.

Blue lights appeared among the blackened contours of the hills. A horse and various corpse candles rose higher along the burial path, not straying to either side of the coffin line for fear of cursing the surrounding farmland. The feet of the body faced uphill in its wooden box, and the horse carried it calmly up the incline among the blue lights until the storm came, when it bolted out of its harness and ran off into the darkness.

The horse galloped through the storm and along the rocky ascent all the way back past Greg's Hut. It carried on west past Cocklock Scar before reaching the churchyard at Kirkland where it whinnied in the moonlight, waking the inhabitants there who rose from their beds to join it in the wind and rain.

In the morning, he drank tea in the hope of calming himself after a troubled night. The wind had rocked at the tent so hard he'd had to spread himself across the groundsheet. He had a vague memory of galloping. He took the tent down and packed it away in his rucksack before walking across to the drystone wall, and when he looked over prior to climbing it, he saw what had been left on a big stone so its spirit wouldn't touch the ground.

TRYFAN

It started in a boozer in Barmouth the night before, and in the morning, we dug out what gear we had and headed for Tryfan. Baz and I hadn't been walking for years, but we'd come to Tryfan once before and been denied an ascent by the rain. On this spring morning, the sun shone across a frosted Wales and ravens croaked in gregarious pairs.

We laboured up along the path, and as with many mountains the path disappeared near the summit and we had to cross slippery boulders and shards of broken stone. Many times, we stopped during the climb. A stonechat came and went. Meadow pipits rolled in waves through the sky.

At the summit the three metre obelisks of Adam and Eve stood before us; beyond them the abyss of the East Face. Baz let me go first. I climbed onto the first obelisk and stood there in the sunlight, buffeted by the breeze. I felt the ache of exposure between the two rocks and looked down the chasm of the sheer face. I took the step across, exhilarated, and as I climbed down relaxation washed over me.

I could tell Baz didn't want to do it. But I was being cocky. It was nothing, I told him, just a small step across. Keep your eye on where you put your feet and don't look down. Baz was shaking as he climbed onto the first rock. I wondered which one was Adam, which one was Eve.

OCEAN

It was hot. I looked through the binoculars as she vacuumed the living room. She wore a white vest and beige jeans. She vacuumed in a determined manner and must have been very warm. She bent over in front of the window both ways. She moved chairs and looked at them before moving them and looking at them again. On the blue of the living room wall was scrawled the word 'ocean'.

RUMSON

Justin walked down the highway, up and over a hill to the train station, and caught the Amtrak to the rural town where the rock star was said to live. At the station, he got a bus closer and asked the driver about the location, and the driver said he didn't know anything about any rock stars. None of the local people he spoke to would admit to knowing where his idol lived. But he had the name of the town and a map of sorts and a whole day before having to head back to New York.

When he saw the street sign he knew he was close. A jogger came down the road, a young man, fresh-faced, breathing lightly despite the vigour of the exercise. Too pumped for second thoughts he blurted out the address.

Justin began to walk more quickly down the centre of the long road. He felt his inside pocket. He reached the wide iron gates and squinted through them but the house was too far down the gravel drive for him to see anything. As he started to walk around the side he heard the camera twitch behind him, and when he reached the gates at the back the camera there picked up his progress. From the back gates, he could see the distant house, and then he began to hear some activity. A couple of Alsatian dogs came running and barking down the gravel path.

Justin felt fear instead of excitement. He walked back around to the front of the house and spoke into an intercom and was told harshly by security to go away. His voice began to break as he told the gruff man that he wasn't there to harm anybody. At that point the voice became much more assertive, telling Justin that if he didn't go away, the dogs, that by now had come running around to the front, would be let out, and that the security man himself would come out too. Justin left the note he'd written on top of the intercom and then made as though to walk away, only to double back and sit on a grass verge by the other side of the road, his eyes trained on the gates, waiting for any car or tour bus or motorbike to come back.

After a few minutes a black and white police car turned up with the red flashlight going around but no siren. The officer stepped out and told Justin to put his hands in the air and then frisked him. Justin smiled and said there was no need and the officer told him to be quiet.

'What's your name, son?'

'Justin.'

'Well, Justin, we've had a call from the security people. We can't have you hanging around here.'

'I just wanted to meet—'

'—Yes, well, there's nobody home, and there's nobody going to be home any time soon. Do you understand?'

'There's no need for all this, honestly, I just—'

'—I said *do you understand?*'

'Yes.'

'Okay now. Don't make me have to come back here.'

'Okay, okay,' said Justin, hanging his head.

'I don't understand you people, I really don't,' said the officer. 'Look, I can drop you at the train station.'

'No, no, it's okay. I'll walk back.'

As he pulled away the officer lowered his window and looked out at Justin. 'Time to get moving, son,' he said, 'don't make me come back here.'

As the police car disappeared it occurred to Justin how he must have looked in the security camera. He had a red beard and wore a woolly hat and a long black coat, and his shoes were muddy. He'd come to a small town in rural America to hang around outside the house of his idol. His idol wasn't even in. Security had told him to go away, the police had come. What the hell was he doing there? Weren't

48

the albums and the books and the bootlegs and the DVD's enough?

At the bus stop on the highway Justin looked across the road and through trees at a line of low hills in the distance.

'Justin?' said a man wearing a baseball cap and sunglasses who'd slowed his '59 Chevrolet to a crawl. 'It's Justin, right?'

'Yeah, yeah.'

'Thanks for the note, man.'

'Okay. Sorry if I caused you any trouble.'

'It's no problem. How's your vacation going?'

'It has been okay. I'm going back tomorrow,' he said, seeing his own face reflected in the sunglasses.

THE MUMS

Kim parked in the usual place and waited for the clock on the dashboard to reach 3:00. Then she took her youngest from the back seat and walked with her across the road at the traffic lights and past the pub and the ice cream van, before standing at the back of the crowd of mums. When the gate opened in the corner of the playground the crowd of mums filtered through. The crowd moved towards the far end of the playground and waited for the classroom door to open. Each child came out, one at a time, the teachers watching to see the boy or girl re-united with their parent. When Kim's little boy appeared, he gave Kim a kiss and then a kiss to his little sister. The three of them turned and made their way back towards the tiny gap of the opened gate in the wire fence and walked back past the ice cream van and the pub to the car. Slowly the voices of the mums quietened as Kim and her children crossed the road at the traffic lights. With her children secured in the car seats, Kim started the engine and put on the radio and began dancing and jigging to the music. She looked in the rear-view mirror with her smiling eyes and watched as her son and daughter started dancing too.

CLASS

The art group met on Friday afternoon as usual. All the women were over the age of seventy. The model was called Johnson. He was Australian and he had a thick brown beard, a very skinny body and shaved genitals.

Every week as the old women sat studying the male form and sketching in their notebooks there was an unspoken expectation twitching in the air. They kept the room very warm to keep the blood circulating. Several of the women suffered from cold feet on a weekly basis but still managed to endure.

Heather was the leader of the group. She'd studied with Norman Ackroyd in the 1960's. She'd also spent many years teaching at the Royal College of Art before moving to Yorkshire.

She had painted many male nudes over the years and not all of them were up for the task. Some didn't know how to follow instruction and pose, while for others it was a natural response that facilitated any number of possible images.

One week a new member of the group came along. Sabina was from Poland and studying at Leeds Metropolitan University. She preferred to use charcoal for her sketches. She was pleased by Johnson and sketched what she saw.

When Heather saw Sabina's drawings she was outraged. Sabina would get a complete refund on the eight weeks on the condition she left the group immediately. Those kinds of drawings were just not welcome.

THE BRIDLEWAY

They left their cars by the canal at Bugsworth Basin and walked past the Navigation and under the two railway bridges next to each other. They followed Dolly Lane up past the pig farm and then crossed a stile into a field before ascending to Over Hill Road. Here they went right and then left before passing through a gate and onto the public bridleway.

The rough stony ground rose higher out of the hollows. They sloshed through mud and the trickle of a stream making its way downhill back past them. The grass in and around the mud was a very deep green and there were no flowers or smells other than the horse dung that littered the ascent.

The drystone walls either side of them were grey and weather-wracked and still solidly standing. They could barely see over them and so they ploughed forward over the rough ground, sloshing through the mud and puddles and rolling up and down on the undulating path. Though it had been walked on by so many before them and would be walked on by so many after, the two of them felt they were the first to walk the bridleway.

When the path rose higher and lifted them a little so that they could glimpse across the drystone walls to the sides, on one side they saw the distant city with its big buildings made tiny, and on the other a field filled entirely with sheep and lambs; the lambs running in groups, sometimes leaping off the ground to high kick before rushing back to their mother to nuzzle roughly at her teats.

Higher still in another field to their right there was a grouping of black cows; black cows steaming and huddled with big soulful eyes following each other's movements. And when the cows spotted them they all followed each other over to their side of the drystone wall, their big eyes watching the two people walking along the bridle pathway.

Further up the bridle pathway there was a horse leaning over the drystone wall, his head made distinctive by a silver blaze. He was soaking wet and left alone there and he looked forlornly at the walking duo, never seeming to believe that they had anything for him. When they approached him he turned away and walked off through the mud on his side of the wall, but they called him back and gave him an apple.

Aeroplanes flew low over the bridleway but their engines were ignored because of the trickling of the water and the ever-present sounds of the playing lambs, and the cows, some of whom called out as the others stood steaming and watching.

Jackdaws flew across the bridleway in unfurling fans of black, calling contentedly among themselves before landing in green fields filled with sheep droppings. A solitary kestrel hovered at a distance.

The rain came harder and harder so that the two people continually slipped on the bridleway. They didn't know that some people had come this way in the past only to be completely blocked off by snow drifts piled against the stile. The rain slicked the stile so the two people had to be careful not to slip as they climbed over it, and they held each other's hands so they wouldn't.

When they turned left off the public bridleway after the stile and carried on uphill across a shifting bed of sphagnum moss, it seemed the moss might suck them under, but they passed over it by following one another's careful course. They continued uphill until they reached a T junction of paths imprinted on grass by years of walking feet, and as they approached it, preoccupied for a moment about direction, they saw before them where the bridleway had lead.

A GOOD NIGHT'S SLEEP GUARANTEED

I was staying on the Quayside in Newcastle. I'd spent the evening in the Slug and Lettuce, nursing a few beers and looking out of the window at the Tyne and The Sage. I walked out of there and into the face of a biting wind off the river and walked the short distance to my hotel in the shadow of the Tyne Bridge.

Opening the door and walking into my room I could see and hear the Tyne Bridge through the single glazed windows. There was a thermostat on the wall. I turned it up. I had a shower and then selected the firmer of the two pillow options for bed. I climbed under the covers, naked and relaxed, listening to the receding hum of the traffic.

I drifted off to sleep thinking of my wife. I saw her face in my dreams. I was woken when the thermostat clicked off. It was just on the wall at the side of the bed. I turned it up even more, and when it clicked off again later, again I was woken. It seemed the only way I would get some sleep would be to turn the thermostat right down. But the reading wouldn't go below 18 degrees.

By this time the traffic on the Tyne Bridge was almost silent. I changed to the softer pillow option and drifted off to sleep again, thinking about the warm body of my absent wife.

In the morning, I could see my breath in front of my face. When I opened the curtains, there was ice on the inside of the windows. I looked at the thermostat, which had remained at 18 degrees. But the radiator was cold to the touch.

I was glad that while booking online I had taken the option of the 'all you can eat' breakfast. I spent an hour in the dining area, the morning sun shining in through the big windows. The third plate of sausages tested the patience of the chef and the capacity of my stomach.

Leaving the hotel in the shadow of the Tyne Bridge I stared into the bitter wind coming off the river. It was the wind that caused my tears.

HOW ARE THE MIGHTY FALLEN

I was in the station bar in Newcastle, looking at the ornate ceiling rather than the numerous TV screens showing the same football match. It wasn't as if the football had any commentary. I was listening to the music of Lady Gaga or Katy Perry, one of those. From my plush leather seat facing the bar I could see the behaviour of the people around it. The barmaid was sure to retain her formal frown, not yet entirely alienated by the people on the other side of the bar. There were the usual men, nursing a beer while waiting for a train, briefcase on the floor between their legs as they stood at the bar. There was the usual old bloke in a hat, sat on a stool just back from the bar and looking like a poet on payday.

One bear of a man sitting at the bar kept hugging other people around him. If a man came to the bar for a drink, he unwittingly invited one of these hugs. The bear was slurring his words just a little bit; I could just hear that above the music. I remembered him. He would be about forty-five by now, his fights for the British and European heavyweight titles a distant memory. I couldn't remember if he'd had a world title shot. With the amount of belts these days I guess he must have.

There was a much younger man standing at the bar and looking down on the bear, and this younger man kept leaving the conversation to talk on his mobile phone. As the younger man talked on the phone, I could see that the bear was still trying to keep the conversation going. The younger man had turned away, and didn't turn around. He kept talking on his phone. Then the bear began to tug at the tail of the younger man's suit. But the younger man steadfastly refused to look around, and instead kept talking on his phone. It occurred to me that the younger man had no idea who the bear was.

The bear then turned on his stool, his face searching around the bar. As his narrowing eyes scanned towards me I looked away and up at the ornate clock, high on the wall. And then I saw my pint, still full. I pulled my scarf together and zipped up my coat, taking my suitcase and leaving the pint.

THE ROSE GARDEN

Quite handy really, it was so close by I didn't even need to get the bus or anything. I'd been past it so many times on the way to school. The first day I didn't do that much except change sheets and mop the floors and listen as they told me time and again about superbugs.

On my second day, I heard someone talk about a 'rosy'. I heard it again, surrounded by crackle on a walkie-talkie. The other porters gave each other knowing looks, enjoying the secret they had over me. I knew they were waiting for me to ask so I held off as long as I could, to deflate their smugness. Don't get me wrong, apart from that, they're a nice bunch of people. I've done loads of jobs and it might seem a bit of a cliché but you can have more of a laugh with people at the lower end of things. Some people just aren't that ambitious, and they are way easier to get on with because they're not up their own arse. Even those in better paid jobs stay in the same place for the same reason. It is easier than starting something new.

I don't care if I get sacked. It's surprising what you can get away with, having that attitude, if it is how you genuinely feel. I don't like telling people what to do, but I don't like being told what to do either. I like knowing what I have to do and getting it done. All the other things are justifications.

They told me at the interview what I would have to do. When I did it, it wasn't as bad as it had been in my imagination. Otto had been there for seventeen years, and he was the bloke who showed me how. The call had come in for a 'rosy', and I walked behind him into the room.

All you see are the sheets and the box. Nobody takes a blind bit of notice when you are taking them where they have to go. The other porters have this standard kind of banter about it every time, as though the fun of keeping the secret outweighs what we have to carry.

But sometimes what we have to carry hardly weighs anything at all. None of us wants to do this one and there are no jokes to cover it up. It takes only one hand which makes it more difficult. Yet nobody ever notices as you pass them with the plastic carry case.

THE PAINTER

She stood on the wooden porch looking out across the water, with all the black and white birds swirling and calling, and she took the steps down and walked through the grass past all her sculptures, and she knew she'd toss it all away for the one she loved all those years before, in those rapid months before experience filled all the tides of the bay with the past. She walked across the shifting sands and right down to the water's edge and into the water, where she paddled with tiny crabs biting at her feet before plunging in, winding in and out between the jellyfish in all their extraordinary colours. In the evening sunlight across the bay, she ran chasing the black and white birds, chasing them until sweat poured down her chest, and then after walking back through the dusk to the studio, she showered and returned to the canvas.

FACTORY

As the boxes ran down the metal slope, the two men in front continued to pick them up and stack them onto pallets, looking at the labels on the boxes and leaving some to roll on to where Corned Beef stood at the end of the line. He looked how the other pallets were stacked and tried to copy, until the man in charge moaned and leaned over to show him the right way. When the pallet was full, the man picked up a roll of shrink-wrap and told Corned Beef to watch as he ran around and around the pallet with it, wrapping it tight before a man on a fork lift truck came over and took the pallet to the storage racks.

After about an hour, and after filling his third pallet with boxes, Corned Beef walked over to the man in charge and said, 'What do we do after this?'

THE STOAT

Snow had covered the moorland all around Willimoteswick Castle so I hadn't been walking for a while. The last time I walked in the snow I'd exhausted myself along Hadrian's Wall, wading through the drifts from one milecastle to another, and all the time looking across at more snowfall approaching from above Wark Forest to the north. I left the wall at turret 38A and made my way to the military road before climbing over a drystone wall and heading back home via High Shield. There were buzzards circling above the Long Stone on Barcombe Hill and I didn't see a soul all day. My legs felt like the snow added another couple of miles to the circuit.

I moved to the village after starting a PhD at Northumbria University, but had kept to myself. I told my neighbour that I worked at the university and word seemed to go around after that. In the countryside, people look at you with wary eyes if they haven't seen you before, but when they see you a second time, often they'll say hello.

When I first met my neighbour John, I made a few jokes. It was something I did when I met people, but it seemed that in this village nobody had a sense of humour. Or if they did it was a humour different to mine. I think it might have been something to do with irony. Nobody in the village seemed to incorporate its possibility. I'd experienced this in the city and the suburbs as well. I'd say something ironic and the person just looked at me blankly.

As a way to find friendship, I tried to be as literal as I could, but with my character being as it is that left me with little to say. I had developed in an environment in Manchester where friendship came about through proximity, and mutual respect based upon one person's ability to undermine the other.

In the countryside in winter I didn't see anyone else for weeks on end. It was dark when I left in the morning and dark when I came back, and there were hardly any streetlights. It was so cold that at weekends, with the wind howling off the moorland, people didn't go anywhere without their cars.

I had solitude on my winter walks. The weather had to be really bad for it to be quiet along the wall, but on the other side of the South Tyne Valley nobody except me used any of the footpaths at all. It wasn't my instinct to join things. There was a walking festival in Haltwhistle but that was my idea of hell. I went walking for peace and quiet, not to listen to people wittering on all day and spoiling beauty by analysing it.

And there was a gardening group at the local park, with signs stuck up on the two lampposts in the village inviting people to help with the development of a woodland trail. These notices always had 'All Welcome' at the bottom of them. I interpreted this not as a sign of friendship, but as a way for them to find out who I was.

In summer during my solitary walks across the moorland around Willimoteswick Castle, I was astonished by the amount of rabbits. There were hundreds and hundreds of them racing across the moorland from one warren to another. Sometimes I'd train my binoculars on what seemed an empty hillside and see hundreds of little brown rabbits all sitting there together. I couldn't distinguish one from the other. Sometimes rabbits would rush past and seem to vanish into thin air as they ran headlong back into their warrens. On country roads, I'd see dozens of rabbits in various stages of decomposition, with their eyes always pecked out by the crows; crows that nested in the tall trees by the side of the A69.

After most of the snow had melted away, causing the burns to roar down from the moorland and raise the river levels beyond the three-metre line under the Millstone Bridge, I headed out onto the moorland above Willimoteswick Castle.

Passing the castle, I crossed the burn and took the bridleway past an enclosure filled with partridge. I climbed higher on a long winding path between grazing sheep. The tarmac gradually disappeared into a grassy track and I crossed a stile into a field near Allensgreen. Walking among pheasants on a tree shaded road I passed the farmhouse along a muddy track and paused by the silver descent of a waterfall. Climbing over the brow of a little hillock, a view of the South Tyne Valley stretched out before me, all the way across to Hadrian's Wall and beyond. The silver river shone in bright curls.

As I walked back down the road and returned past the castle, I was stopped in my tracks by a white wave in susurrations along the tarmac. Reaching into my rucksack I took my binoculars out and trained them onto the stoat, which was bright white against the greens and browns and blacks of the winter scene. It stood up on its hind legs to survey the muddy terrain of the fields on either side of the road, then lowered itself and ran a little, before stopping and surveying the scene again. I had made previous mistakes with nature, taking out my camera to try and get a picture and in doing so missing the moment, so this time I just watched the stoat, fixing my binoculars on its movements. I inched slowly along the road and got closer and closer, adjusting the binoculars as I went to capture the white stoat in its winter image. I couldn't believe I could get so close, but the stoat was so preoccupied with its own observations that it didn't seem to see me at all. I was upwind of it and kept watching, so transfixed I didn't notice the ache in my arms from holding the binoculars. When I did feel them aching I lowered the binoculars for a moment, and when I looked through them again the stoat had gone. I rushed down the road to where it had been and scanned the fields on either side, but I never saw the stoat again.

What made it such a special moment for me was that I hadn't known what it was when I saw it; before that moment I didn't know that such a creature existed. It was then that I thought of the buzzards in the sky; those buzzards looking down on a stoat that stood out so brightly from its surrounds. And I thought that the stoat wouldn't last long unless it learned to shed its winter coat at the same time as the snow began to melt.

FOG LANE

When I was a kid I used to watch my brother playing for the local football team and in most games, you couldn't see from one set of goalposts to another. It was the same on the lane; a long straight road disappearing into the mist.

It was on the lane and in the park that I made most of my money. Dog walkers, old people and innocents were my target, and it was so easy to bump an elbow, grab a purse and drift off into the mist. I did about fifty in a fortnight until they got me. It was a CSO that identified me from the line-up.

There was this one time I mugged an old lady. She limped along with a wooden stick and I had to hold her up while I robbed her. Poor cow had her life savings on her. It was a few grand and I was permanently high for a while there.

She came to see me in prison. It was a thing they did to make you face the victims of your crime. I asked her why she carried her life savings around with her and she said it was safer than leaving the money in the house. She didn't trust the bankers either. I thought she should hate me, but I came to realize that she welcomed the chance to come and talk. They told me she had Alzheimer's and not to worry if she talked to me like I was her daughter. I said I'd go and see her when I got out but it was too late by then. She didn't even know who I was.

RAINBOW SNOOKER CLUB

Two people were having sex at the back of The Hacienda. Tom continued past them along the canal towpath and came out near The Peveril of the Peak. He tried the locked doors of the Briton's Protection. He looked through the frosted glass at the drinkers sat at the bar and then wandered towards Whitworth Street. In the shadow of Oxford Road Station there was a girl sitting on the steps of The Rainbow Snooker Club.

'Spare some change? she asked, holding out a plastic cup.

He reached into his trouser pocket, pulled out a fistful of heavy change and passed her some pound coins. 'I recognize you. You're Kelly Brown. Don Brown's sister.'

'So what?'

'Well what are you doing here?'

'Spare some change?' she said, as a man in a suit walked past.

'Do you want to go in for a game of snooker?'

'Don't be daft.'

'Is there a bar in there?'

'Of course there is.'

'Can I buy you a drink?'

'Come on then.'

Smoke carried across the tables from the barman's cigarette but nobody played snooker. The old man was reading a *Manchester Evening News*, the newspaper spread out across the bar.

Tom stood with Kelly. The barman eventually looked up. Kelly looked at Tom. 'What do you want?' Tom said.

'Jack Daniels and coke.'

'Jack Daniels and coke? Okay mate, two of those.'

She drank hers in one. Then she told Tom she was going.

'Why? Where to? Come on, let me get you another. I've got plenty of money, don't worry about that.'

'George, can you do us a cup of tea?' she said to the barman.

'Tea?' said Tom.

'Yeah, tea.'

When George passed her the tea she took the mug in two hands and brought it close to her chest. Tom had a Jack Daniels with ice.

'Let's have a game.'

'What?'

'Let's have a game of snooker.'

'You're too pissed.'

'I'm not,' he said. 'I'll get a lager. Sure you don't want one?'

'Sure.'

He passed her a cue and she stood there watching as he tried to get the reds in the triangle. He put the green on the yellow spot but apart from that it was right. When he broke off he completely missed the pack. He walked over to the scoreboard on the wall and slid it to 4.

She walked to the table. But she couldn't hold the cue properly and with her first shot she brushed the side of the white with the cue tip, moving it a few inches and not hitting any other ball. George carried on reading the paper.

'Stupid game this,' she said, after missing another shot.

'You are useless,' he said, laughing at her.

'Get yourself another drink.'

'I will. And you drink your tea.'

He managed a decent break. Then she missed and he made another break to take the frame. He was getting into it and wanted to play more but she was bored.

After a frame on his own he got himself another lager. They left the snooker club and trailed around the

Manchester streets, before spending some time in a cafe on Piccadilly Approach, around the corner from The Waldorf. She had more tea and he had some too but it made him feel sick. He wanted another drink and she told him where they could get one if he just followed her.

He couldn't remember finishing that last drink. He didn't remember what had happened to the girl, or the money in his pockets, but he supposed there was a connection.

THE ROAD TO ECCLES

I had never been loved before. And I'd never had someone fall out of love with me before. I thought when someone was in love that was it. Seems I was wrong. He left me a load of his CDs so maybe that's why I still love him.

I moved into the first half-decent looking flat I could find. It was fine except for the bellicose lesbians upstairs and the fact that I was on the ground floor. Because of being on the ground floor I heard the front door bang every time it closed. Morning and night, I was woken by this closing door. I moved the bed to the furthest corner of the room and dragged the wardrobe over to where the bed had been. Then I piled as much stuff as I could into the wardrobe. It made no difference. The door woke me every morning at 6.55, 7.25, and 7.55. Add on ten minutes to each of those and you'll get the train times into town.

I began to relieve my misery by eating Eccles Cakes. Not Chorley Cakes, Eccles Cakes. I preferred the pastry. They came in packets of four and at first I would only eat the occasional cake in company. Then I started to eat them on my own. Every Friday night I would eat all four, one after the other. I'd drag myself to bed alone and lie there stroking by bloated belly. One morning I woke on the floor with pastry all down my front. The night before I'd made my way through two packets while listening to *Ladies of the Canyon*.

THE HOUSE SITTER

The strange cat next to him is staring, her eyes bright green in the dusk. He looks out through the long windows. The light through the balcony on the side of the big house opposite continues to fade. The sun falls away. A goldfinch lands on a telephone wire and sits there without moving. From behind it has the shape of a bell. The windows are open. There's the sound of blackbirds protecting their nest. He looks down at his gut. Silver droplets of sweat are going grey. There are dancing lights on the alarm of the house opposite. They dance right to left, left to right. Rapid footsteps approach and then fade. They come back and fade again. His right hand reaches slowly across to the beer bottle as light rain leaves scratches on the window glass.

They were there and then they were gone. A fortnight in Barbados, something like that. The door closed behind them all and then he was in there alone. He had never tried Netflix before. He put it on and searched through all the films for something he knew. He watched *Jackie Brown*. What a woman.

He walked the rooms. Three floors and a cellar. Four bathrooms, yes, four bathrooms. He took a dump in each one and didn't flush. He washed his hands, dried them, and dropped the towels to the floor. He heard the soft brush of footsteps behind him. The green eyes shone on the cool wooden floor. He rubbed his cock and kept walking.

There were books he didn't know. Records he couldn't play. Coffee he couldn't make. Picture frames without pictures, lipsticks without lips. He walked across the patio, his feet cracking the shells of snails. He walked into the garden and fell to his knees. He gripped at the herbs, ripping them out of the ground, and then turned and lay on his back below the blazing July sun. Beside him was the plastic circle of an empty pond.

71

Dark now, he walks the rooms again. He sits down on the rug in the living room, his body distorted in the reflection from the switched off TV. It sits in a black baize before him. The piss sinks into the rug and leaves a spreading blotch. He gets up and walks down to the cellar without switching on the light. His feet bruise a little on the cold stone floors where the concrete has set in ripples. Passing the washing machine and dryer and a shelf filled with nails and glue he walks into a room filled with pigeons. They shift and shatter and shit. Flying around his head, they hit each other mid-flight and fall. Feathers fall away and land on the blue floor.

Searing pain surges from his big toe. He limps to one of the four bathrooms. There are no longer any muscles on his arms. His swollen belly pushes at the mirror. There is a razor there, at the side of the sink. He looks at his beer gut and then back up at his beard.

He walks to one of the front bedrooms and looks through the window. Silver slug trails criss-cross the driveway where there is room for two cars to park off road. The 'Flat to Let' sign remains next door, red lettering on white board. Polish men carry planks of wood inside. There is constant drilling and hammering and banging and sawing. It is a haunted house of peeling brown paint and swollen windows, twelve separate studio flats housing single men and women at £350 a month. If he looks sideways, he can see into one of the windows. A young woman sits before a wooden dresser applying make-up. He watches her until she is finished and then he moves away from the window, his neck sore and aching. In the living room, he searches Netflix again. He watches *Donnie Brasco* while drinking bottles of Coors Light.

Jura campsite. The haunted scraping sounds of short-eared owls in the night, like the sound of tearing plastic. And then the sounds from the distillery, and the oystercatchers and curlews in the bay. But most of all the throaty scraping sounds of the short eared owls at night.

Four fifty am. Sunlight hits the tent walls. He zips open the door, looks out across the bay. Clouds have covered the sun. He pisses on the grass among a spray of midges. She won't leave the tent. He puts on his midge hood and fills a pan of water from the burn. He puts it on the stove to boil. Swallows flash and glide and swoop and feast in the midge-filled morning.

They pack up and fill their panniers. Then they cover themselves in midge hoods that reach down to their waists and cycle the long road back to the Feolin Ferry, where they hand their dampened tickets to the ferryman. Back on Islay, he stops for a moment to ask her about the wisdom of carrying on. She says nothing and cycles straight on to the ferry back to the mainland.

On the journey there, they had marvelled at the Paps of Jura, the quartzite rock glistening under a cloudless blue sky. He had run down the charger on his phone by taking so many pictures. It was only when he looked back at them that he realized he had taken none of her.

It was while they were drinking Jura Suspicion, one of a variety of single malt whiskies produced by the island distillery. A death was contained, somewhere in an ill-chosen phrase. The football continued on the TV. It was the World Cup. Later they chatted to a German guy from the campsite. He was cycling too. He looked like a cross between Richard E Grant and Rutger Hauer, and said he was going to Colonsay.

He comes back with another crate of Coors Light. After watching *The Color of Money* on Netflix he lies on the couch in the living room, looking out through the long windows at the dancing alarm, and the light fading behind the balcony. There are the brightening green eyes of the cat. Rapid footsteps come and go on the pavement outside. Droplets of sweat cool on his body as he sleeps, and he wakes to the shrieking of the short eared owls.

THE TAP AND SPILE

There was a woman at the hairdressers in Hexham. He'd sit there waiting his turn and she would bend over in tight jeans and her arse was almost in his face. She had bottle red hair and was from Prudhoe.

They'd go to the little cinema in Hexham when she could get a babysitter and he'd see her off when she got on the train back. After a while she introduced him to her little boy. It was a big moment and he had to think about whether he was serious about her.

He was thirty-five then and it was the first time he knew he liked kids. He used to lie there in bed at night thinking about her and he thought that he could make a life with her and her little boy. All the time she was telling him what an arsehole the lad's father was and how she needed someone reliable. Then he saw them together outside the Tap and Spile on Battle Hill. They were drunk and she was clinging on to him.

He always got the train to work. In winter, it was dark there and back so he couldn't appreciate the views along the South Tyne Valley. All he could see in the window was his own reflection. He squinted past that into blackness. But travelling every day he got to know the tiniest lights on the most distant farmhouses, and then the train would start braking, and move slowly over the level crossing. He'd step off into cold and wind and rain and walk up the hill back to the house. He ached for the sight of those jeans in Bob's Barber's, but one day after work he nipped into the Eldon Square shopping centre and bought himself some hair clippers.

He had been following the football season on the radio, and it all came down to the last game of the season at home to Q.P.R. He was pacing around. At two-one down he turned it off. But he had to turn it on again. And when Aguero scored he shouted as loud as he could. After the result sank in he looked around at the empty house and the lovely view of the hills and thought, what the fuck am I doing here?

MONG

I took some agency work as a note taker at a place in Rochdale, taking notes for a young deaf girl called Emma. I hadn't been in a college environment for years.

The morning passed without incident, and I went out through the barriers to enjoy the spring sunshine and pick up some lunch. I sat on a bench beneath the neo gothic splendour of the town hall, eating the two pies I'd bought from Gregg's and washing them down with a large tea. As I'd walked through the town centre I had seen dozens of young girls pushing prams. There seemed to be a childbirth epidemic in the town.

The kids in the class were being prepared for the workplace, picking up literacy skills they'd missed out on at school. They were being prepared as good citizens; good, conforming citizens. There was too much life in some of them for that.

I made notes on the support worker laptop but was dismayed by the teaching standards, especially since I would have killed for such a job myself.

In one of the classes the lecturer set a group exercise based on the question, *'why do you think they have built the new hospital in the town centre?'* The lecturer then gave them twenty minutes to work on it. After half an hour, the lecturer was still looking at her phone. The kids had stopped talking about the hospital long ago, and many of them were also on their phones.

Finally, the lecturer asked them to give feedback on the group exercise. There was a young girl from Rossendale, and she had an endearingly broad Lancashire accent. I had chatted to her briefly, and had overheard her talking all morning. She was about five feet tall and worked behind a bar. She was eighteen but looked closer to twelve. When she spoke you immediately realized she was eighteen after all. 'We don't know. Nobody knows,' she said.

Why don't you know? I've given you twenty minutes. At least twenty minutes.'

'The note taker doesn't even know,' she said, pointing at me.

'I'm not allowed to join in. It is not my job.'

'You mong,' she said. At this point the kids burst out laughing but the lecturer looked seriously alarmed.

'No, no, no,' said the Rossendale girl. 'I don't mean mong in the way you mean it. Not the old way. It is a Rochdale thing.'

'That is not an acceptable word,' said the lecturer, animated – but too late. 'We don't use words like that.'

'Okay but it weren't meant in the way you thought.'

'Any more feedback then on the group task? Why do we think the new hospital has been built in the town centre?'

'I bet you don't even know, Miss.'

I was getting bored, and though I shouldn't have, I piped in with, 'She wouldn't set an exercise or ask a question if she didn't know the answer.' I wasn't being sarcastic, although that is a significant element of my personality.

'I thought you said you weren't allowed to join in,' said the Rossendale girl.

'Don't be a mong,' I said. And all the kids laughed, and it was meant as a joke. I was just so bored. I'd been a naughty kid at school, and even though that was many years before the classroom setting seemed to make me revert to type. The rest of the lesson passed without incident, and the lecturer didn't give an answer for why the new hospital had been built in the town centre. I smiled to her on the way out, as a way to say sorry for adding to the disruption.

But when I got back on the tram I felt a bit sad for those kids. They were being short changed in that college. In that class anyway. The kids were not motivated and the lecturer seemed to get away with being shit. Nobody complains about the lecturer at that age or in that environment. The kids don't know that they can.

The next morning, I got on the tram heading back to Rochdale. There was still a week left on the temporary contract and I needed the money. I was on the tram for ages. I forget exactly where it was, but there was a stretch of the tram line that ran through marshland between low hills. More than once I'd seen the flashing brown of a kestrel in the skies there, and now I spotted it perched on a wire.

I got off the tram and walked past the town hall on my way to the campus. I let myself into the building with my swipe card. As I went to the student support office to pick up the laptop the staff in there didn't seem as friendly as they had been. Then I had a call on my phone.

'Hello?' I said.

'I need you to leave the campus right now.'

'I'm sorry?'

'I need you to leave the campus right now.'

'Why? Who is this?'

'It is Veronica from Hunt Education.'

'But I'm here. I've just come an hour on the tram. What is this about?'

Just then Emma appeared outside. I didn't know sign language but I did my best to communicate to her. She seemed lost. Instead of integrating with the rest of the class I had noticed that she sat on her own at break times, and between classes would always wait around outside the student support office. There was normally an interpreter around who would walk with her to class, but she travelled from the Wirral and hadn't arrived yet.

'Veronica, I've got the student here in front of me.'

'I need you to leave the campus.'

'But why?'

'I'm not prepared to discuss this over the phone.'

EVERYTHING IS SEEN AT ITS BEST IN THE DARK

Sometimes in autumn when the ash trees are filled with red berries there are loads of crows among the branches, and evening sunlight filters through the taller trees, spraying the meadow with golden light. Sue always sits at the same bench near the pond so she can listen to the whispering of the reeds. She's seen whole families of herons by that little pond. And it is quiet down there in the late afternoon. From the bench by the pond she can look beyond the river towards the high rise flat where she lives. And from the eleventh-floor Denis can keep an eye on her too. Denis has always kept his eye on her, but he doesn't know everything. She has friends on Chiffon Way and Angora Drive, and sometimes she sees them in the Old Pint Pot, but mainly it's just her and Denis.

To get to the meadow she cuts down the cycle route instead of going via Blackburn Street. She must be careful to cross on the sharp curve of road. On this occasion a car stops for a stray collie dog that clearly has somewhere to be. Sue crosses and looks up at the apple tree in one of the back gardens down there. She's never seen a cyclist on the route and the road is scattered with broken glass. She follows the road around and finds herself by the bridge. She looks down at the swans that gather beneath it. The water is so shallow she can see tyres on the river bed. She follows along the river by the backs of houses, looking upriver at the weir that sparkles and crashes. She takes a right and then a left past the new houses, where a woman tending a newly-laid lawn ignores her as she walks slowly by. The people in the new houses don't seem to know that it is okay to say 'hello'. Sue thinks of how people are in such a rush these days. She was the same when she was younger, but she has forgotten.

She is not out of breath by the time she reaches the bench by the pond. That is the advantage of coming every day. She concentrates, and listens as the reeds brush together. Then she hears the crows calling out. They fly in pairs above the new-mown grass. How wonderful it must be to fly. It doesn't matter to them if a lift breaks down. In a matter of seconds, a crow can move from the meadow to the roof of the high rise.

When her boy was young, Sue stayed at home with him. When he was a baby he was wonderful, but on some days, the flat could feel like a prison and the panoramic views seemed like a curse. Once, when watching the Telle-Tubbies, she thought she might be going mad. She had nobody to help her. Lee was so tiring in his need for her attention. On nice days, when he was older, they would walk over to the meadow with a football. If they didn't have the football, Lee would just run headlong into the bushes. Once she thought he was going to end up in the pond, he just ran straight towards it. But he loved the football. She remembered when he dribbled it all the way around the park. Even then he was determined. If he set his mind to something he would do it, and there was never any changing his mind. Denis tried to argue, but Sue just showed support. Sometimes she reproaches herself for that.

The friends who did speak were as bad as the ones who didn't. She came to think that condolences are not for the benefit of the bereaved. At first, she hated the sight of poppies at the memorial on Chapel Street. She didn't say anything. Friends said she'd 'come round'. But the years after that were just a blur of keeping busy. They didn't mellow her. She thought of all that pomp and ceremony. For her it was a token gesture. And the patterns kept repeating, and year after year they kept sending the boys and girls of Salford overseas.

Sometimes she thinks Lee might still come back. Sometimes she thinks she sees him in the Old Pint Pot, but there are many young men with broad shoulders and black hair. Sometimes she doesn't remember that he wouldn't look so young now. She always sees him as he was on the day he left. That day when Denis was so proud, and the buttons were brightly shining, and Sue smiled though she wanted to cry. Some days she sees him everywhere. She sees him in Denis's face every night and every day, but that is a good thing.

The whispering of the reeds continues. In the vivid light of dusk, the outline of the crows seems sharpened. As the day descends, their outline blurs, and soon enough they are flying beyond her sight. She buttons her jacket against the cold and begins the walk back. In the darkness, she can hear the wing strokes of the crows. Looking up at the sprinkled lights of the high rise, she can see a darkened figure in the living room window.

At Adelphi Street, she goes right and walks towards the main road. She cuts through the car park and makes her way down the steps and into the Old Pint Pot. She doesn't see the fusilier on Chapel Street, standing in stone. There are no names of any soldiers on that memorial anyway, and she knows nothing about South Africa.

The pub is filled with students. Sue likes them. And they've done up the Old Pint Pot since the last time she came in. They've done a good job with it. She sees Ken and Pauline from Angora Drive. She takes her red wine over to their table by the window. From there she can see the crescent of the Irwell, and beyond that, the moonlight shining across the meadow.

HERE COMES THE SUN

I was walking down the corridor listening to trombones. I picked up the urinal cakes from the store closet, knocked on the toilet door and walked in. A student was in there so I stepped back out and waited by the door. When he came out I went and dropped the cakes into the urinals and went back out for the mop and bucket. I put the little yellow sign up outside the door and then went in and mopped the bogs before signing my name on the sheet on the wall.

As I headed back towards the store room with the mop and bucket I could hear more music coming from one of the rooms along the corridor. Someone was playing George Harrison's 'Here Comes the Sun' on a flute.

When I was a kid I had this band. And we played in clubs all over town, even got to play some festivals. But they left us out of pocket. Like, for example, the South by Southwest Festival in Austin, Texas. We had to pay our way out there and back and we didn't get paid for playing there and we lived on cheeseburgers for two days and lived in a Super 8 motel which seemed like a shithole to me. And the Austin we saw was full of druggies. There were a thousand bands on at the festival and when we played it seemed like everyone was just walking past rather than watching.

That was our Woodstock, and when we came back none of us could be arsed any more. There were loads of bands better than us and we knew it, but I don't know, there was this one time after one of our early gigs when we had to break back into our rehearsal room because we got back too late, and all of us were pushing and shoving at those gates until the padlock finally broke off, and that night as we dropped off our gear it felt like we were part of something.

One day we had an interview on the local radio. When I looked at the figures for the podcast I realized only six people had listened. Yet that had been a great day. Someone asking you about your influences and ambitions.

I sold my guitar on eBay. Fender Stratocaster. I got hardly anything for it but there are bills to pay. The kids are fine, they're used to the way it is, don't know different. But I worry about the damp in the corner of our bedroom ceiling, hope it doesn't spread. Billy the kid has asthma already and I can't help thinking that was something to do with the house.

So, about this porter job. I had to take it. This guy told me it was easy and he told me that I had more chance as an English guy because none of the other porters were English. He said they were mostly Polish or from Zimbabwe. And they are, but they are good lads, and women too. The Polish are grafters. And my best mate at work is Togara, who comes from Harare.

There was this strike by the lecturers, so all the classes were off. And on that day, I went in one of the rooms up on the second floor. I was emptying out all the waste paper bins. The bins in the classrooms were fine. They call them seminars but I just call them classrooms. It's the bins in the lecturer's rooms that are the worst. Soggy tea bags, crisp packets, chocolate wrappers. So anyway, I was in this classroom and I was just putting a new liner in the waste bin when I saw an acoustic guitar there. Few quid's worth. I don't know why but I started into playing 'Wish You Were Here' by Pink Floyd. And this guy came in.

'Err... what do you think you are doing?' he said.

'Oh sorry, mate, someone left it out.'

'Well that's not your job, is it?'

'Sorry, who are you again?'

'I'm a lecturer here. I have been for many years.'

'Shouldn't you be on strike?'

'Excuse me?'

'I thought you were all out on strike today. Because you only got a one percent pay rise or something.'

'That's right.'

'Why aren't you on strike then?'

'Since you ask, I don't follow the crowd.'

'Fair play.'

'I mean; you didn't get a pay rise, did you?'

'Nah, chief, we've been on the same wages for about six years now. And we do a load of stuff we didn't have to before. More work for the same money. But what are you going to do? There's no jobs out there. You have to stick with the job you've got. And they know it.'

'Well there's no arguing with that. That's why I've come in today.'

'Well it's not for me to say, chief. Your choice. Your family.'

'You know you really shouldn't be in here.'

'Oh come on, chief. There's nobody around today. Who's going to know?'

'I have assignments to mark.'

'You can have a break, can't you? What do you teach?'

'Classical music.'

'Why? Can't you play anything?'

'It's not about if I can play anything.'

'Listen, chief, come and have a listen to this. Do you know Pink Floyd?'

'I've heard of them, yes.'

'This is a song about Syd Barrett and about the music business but there's more to it than that.'

'Syd Barrett?'

'He was in the band when they started,' I said, and I played the opening chords again, and this old boy pulled out a chair and sat down and watched me. When he saw I could play he started listening to the lyrics too. He took off his glasses and his face looked kinder. Kind of vulnerable too, squinting. He rubbed his eyes. I don't know what he was thinking about. He mumbled something about his wife. I showed him the chords and he said he was going to try to play it when he got home.

Geoff, that was his name. I never noticed him before that day. There's talk of them knocking this building down, moving everyone to the new building. Won't be the same. I've got a gig in my local on Monday night. There's two for one on burgers.